NOEMI

BEAR
WITH ME

EERDMANS BOOKS FOR YOUNG READERS
GRAND RAPIDS, MICHIGAN

There's nothing you can do
when a bear comes to stay.

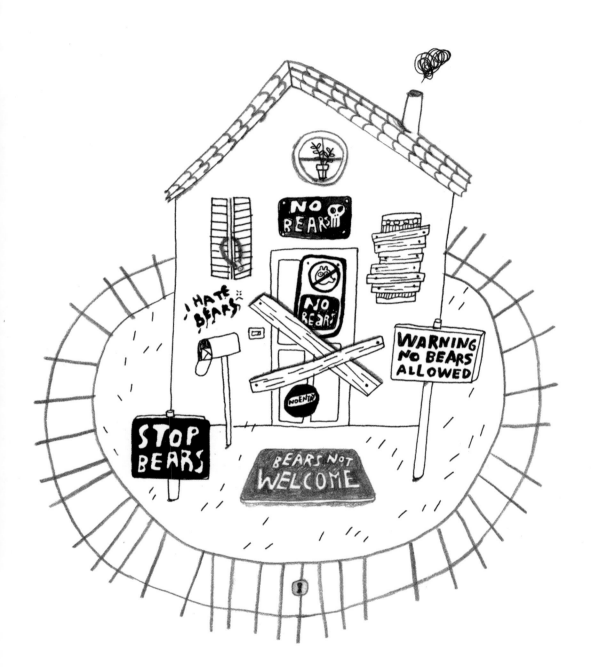

He simply shows up.

And I'm not talking about any old bear,
but the very worst bear on the whole entire planet.

The most ugly, fat, fierce, nasty, annoying,
naughty, hairy, horrible, rude, out-of-place,
demanding, in-the-way, scruffy, bucktoothed,
unwelcome, party-pooping, holiday-wrecking,
cookie-stealing, ignorant coward . . .
you get the gist.

Ultimately, a total

DISA

STER.

(Plus, I'm allergic
to his super stupid fur
that always makes my eyes water.)

So, the first thing I did was to ask him to leave,
in my nicest voice.

PRETTY PLEASE, GO AWAY. THANK YOU!

But good manners are a waste of time with bears.
Bad manners, too.

There's nothing to be done.

You can't run away,

not even really far.

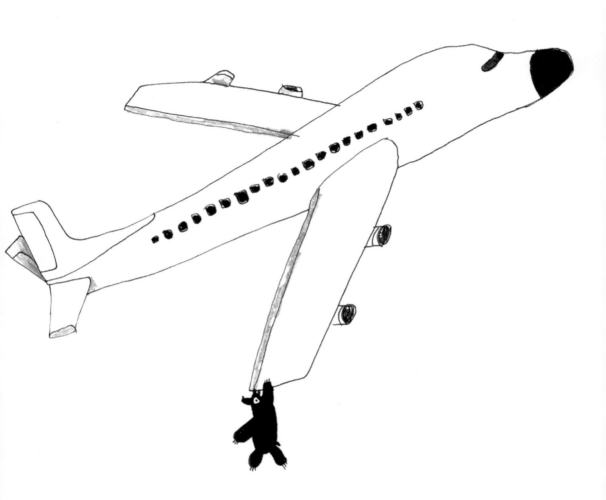

Changing planets would be pointless . . .

. . . because bears ALWAYS know
where you're going,
even when
you don't have a clue.

It would be much easier and far less tiring to surrender,
and simply become his lunch.

But he is so mean that he won't even do you
the favor of eating you.

THE THING IS,
I NEVER WANTED
A BEAR LIKE
THIS →
NOT ONE BIT.

(I HATE BEARS.)

There is no direction,

angle,

40°

or perspective

that makes me like the look of him.

Since he's been here,

things have changed.

Even normal things

like sleeping,

going on vacation,

doing the shopping,

watching a movie,

or hanging out with friends.

This bear, he never leaves me alone.

Except every once in a while,
he follows butterflies or other tiny things,
and he wanders away for a bit.

Sometimes I forget he's here,

and other times, he's the one
who pretends he isn't around.

Once, when we were very tired,
we fell asleep together,
and the next morning he was gone.
He went out alone,
probably looking for a butterfly,
without even staying for breakfast.

Then, as usual,
he came back.

And even now,
he wouldn't reply when I asked him
why he came here to my house
on that one day out of a hundred,
and if he thought it was right,
and why he didn't change his mind,
and if he didn't just get fed up,
and why he didn't care less
about the fact that I hate him
and he will never be my friend,
and that is
FOR SURE.

He just looked at me
the way he always does,
without saying a word.

But what do you expect a bear to say?
I guess that's just how they are.

NOEMI VOLA has a degree in comics and illustration from the Academy of Fine Arts in Bologna. The original edition of *Bear with Me* was exhibited at the Frankfurt Book Fair and the Bologna Book Fair. This book is her North American debut.

Noemi lives in Italy. Visit her blog at noemivola.tumblr.com or follow her on Instagram @volanoemi.

First published in the United States in 2021
by Eerdmans Books for Young Readers,
an imprint of Wm. B. Eerdmans Publishing Co.
Grand Rapids, Michigan

www.eerdmans.com/youngreaders

© Noemi Vola © Maurizio Corraini S.r.l.
All rights reserved to Maurizio Corraini S.r.l. Mantova.
Un orso sullo stomaco 1st Italian edition Maurizio Corraini S.r.l. 2017

English-language translation © Eerdmans Books for Young Readers 2021

Manufactured in Italy

29 28 27 26 25 24 23 22 21   1 2 3 4 5 6 7 8 9

ISBN 978-0-8028-5578-7

A catalog record of this book is available from the Library of Congress.

Illustrations created with pencil and tempera

FSC
www.fsc.org
MIX
Paper from
responsible sources
FSC® C021437